graphix PRESENTS:

GOOSEBUMPS

SLAPPY'S TALES OF HORROR

Adapted and illustrated by Dave Roman,
Jamie Tolagson, Gabriel Hernandez, and Ted Naifeh

Color by Jose Garibaldi

graphix

An imprint of
SCHOLASTIC

HELLO, SLAVES!
You're probably wondering why I've brought you here. It's not for anything pleasant, I can assure you. Well, it's pleasant for me, because I get to see you tremble with dread.
HA-HA-HA!
I've prepared four spine-tingling tales of horror to fuel your nightmares! Now, you may think you can look away, you may think you can escape, but you can't. All you can do is try to make it to the end of this book without going mad from fear!
Our first story, A SHOCKER ON SHOCK STREET, is a happy little tale of terror and mayhem set in a not-so-amusing amusement park. Prepare yourself for the ride of your life... or death!
HA-HA-HA-HA!!!

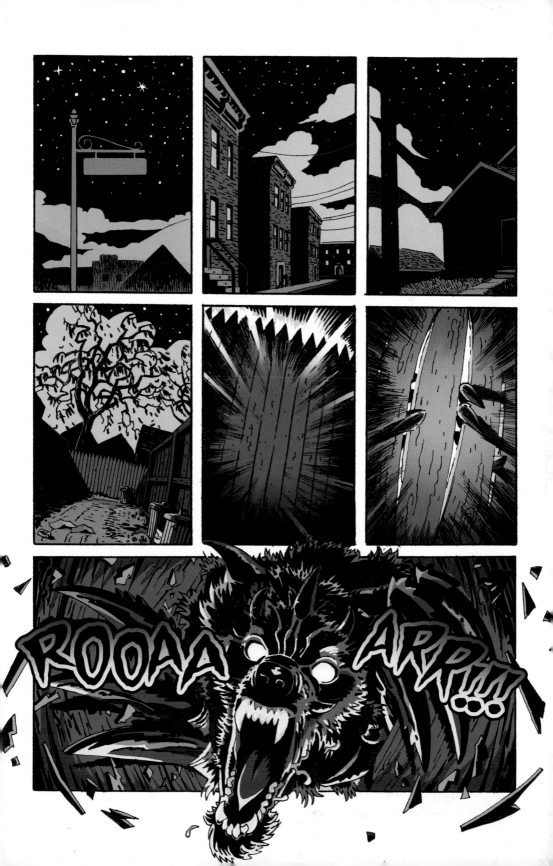

3

6

...IT WILL BE USED AT THE *SHOCKER STUDIO TOUR.*

YOU'VE BEEN WORKING ON THE TOUR FOR FOUR YEARS. IS IT FINALLY GOING TO OPEN?

YES. BUT BEFORE IT DOES, I WANT YOU TWO TO TEST IT OUT.

YOU MEAN IT?

YES! YES! YES!

DAD, THE *SHOCK STREET* MOVIES ARE THE *BEST!* AWESOME! IS IT SCARY?

THE *REAL SHOCK STREET?* YOU GET TO RIDE DOWN THE REAL STREET WHERE THEY MAKE THE MOVIES?

YES. THE REAL SHOCK STREET, AND I WANT YOU TO GO BY YOURSELVES. I THINK THAT WILL MAKE IT MORE EXCITING FOR YOU.

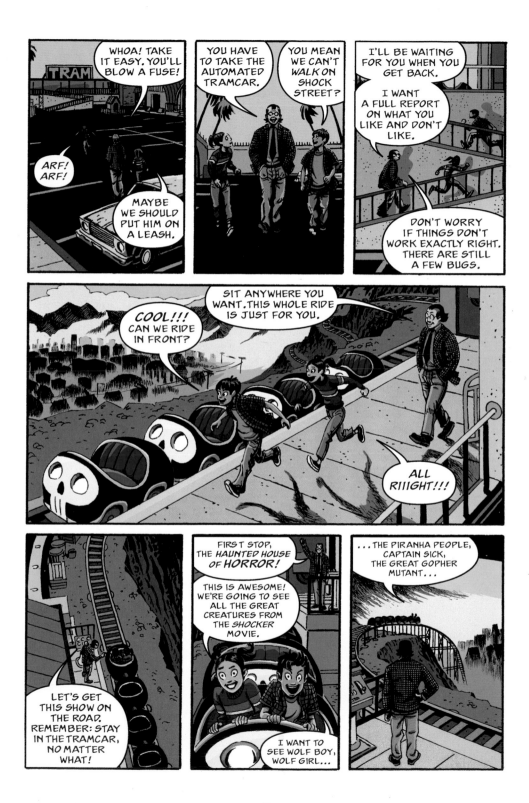

10

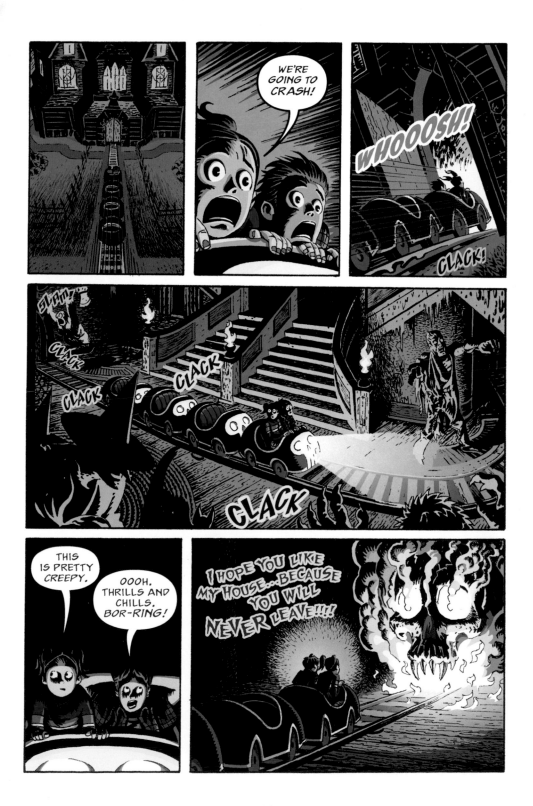

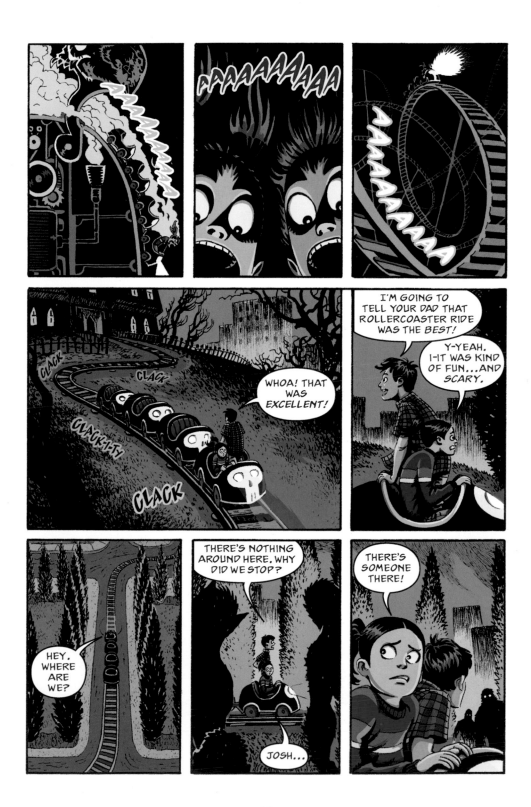

14

16

19

21

26

28

30

31

33

35

THE END

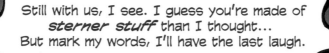

IT ALL BEGAN WHEN WE MOVED TO **FLORIDA.**

I CAN STILL HEAR MY DAD TELLING US THIS WAS THE CHANCE OF A LIFETIME, AN **ADVENTURE** WE'D NEVER FORGET.

HE COULDN'T HAVE KNOWN BACK THEN HOW RIGHT HE WAS!

47

EMILY! WAIT UP! HE'S CHASING US!

RUN, GRADY, RUN!

HEY, THIS LOOKS FAMILIAR. LET'S GO!

51

AAAAOOOUUUU

AFTER BREAKFAST THE NEXT MORNING, I LED DAD OUT TO THE BACKYARD. WHEN I SAW WHAT WAS LYING IN A HEAP ON THE GRASS, I STARTED TO GAG.

IT WAS A **RABBIT** THAT HAD BEEN RIPPED OPEN, NEARLY TORN IN HALF.

I'M GLAD THE DEER ARE SAFE INSIDE THAT PEN.

WOLF!

WOOF!
WOOF!
WOOF!

WOLF, DOWN! HA, HA HA!

YOUR DOG IS A **KILLER.**

64

I'M AFRAID YOUR DOG IS A KILLER.

THAT WAS DUMB, GRADY.

WOLF WILL COME BACK LATER. WHEN HE DOES, I'LL HAVE TO TAKE HIM AWAY.

BUT, DAD—

NO MORE DISCUSSION.

COME HELP ME GET THE DEER PEN PATCHED UP.

ALL DAY LONG, I WATCHED THE SWAMP. I FELT NERVOUS, SHAKY.
BY EVENING, WOLF HADN'T RETURNED.

MY WHOLE FAMILY WAS TENSE. AT DINNER, WE HARDLY SPOKE.

I WENT TO BED EARLY. I WAS REALLY TIRED FROM BEING UP MOST OF THE NIGHT BEFORE.

IT WAS THE LAST NIGHT OF THE FULL MOON, BUT HEAVY BLANKETS OF CLOUDS COVERED THE MOONLIGHT.
I SETTLED MY HEAD INTO THE PILLOW AND TRIED TO SLEEP.

THEN THE HOWLS STARTED...

THAT WAS A MONTH AGO.

THE LAST THING I REMEMBER THEN IS SEEING **WILL** RUN AWAY ON ALL FOURS. **WOLF** FOLLOWED.
I HEARD WILL UTTER A CRY OF PAIN, A WAIL OF DEFEAT.

I SANK DOWN INTO BLUE-BLACK DARKNESS . . .

. . . AND WOKE UP IN MY OWN BEDROOM.

HOW—HOW DID I GET HERE?

WILL WAS GONE.

BUT I KNOW I'LL NEVER FORGET HIM. **HE CHANGED MY LIFE.**

I'M STANDING AT MY BEDROOM WINDOW NOW, WATCHING THE FULL MOON RISING THROUGH THE TREES.

CASSIE WAS RIGHT. WHEN A WEREWOLF BITES YOU, HE PASSES ON **THE CURSE.**

AAAOOOOUUUU

THE END

Well, well, well. You survived after all. No matter. There's more where that came from! HA-HA!
Here lies Dear Reader RIP

Here lies Dear Reader RIP
Next we have a tale of *ghastly woe* to make even the toughest person quake with fear. The title is *GHOST BEACH,* and it's a scream!
So read on, if you *dare*. Just don't come crying to me when it gets to be too much!

I DON'T REMEMBER HOW WE GOT TO THE GRAVEYARD.

THE SKY GREW DARK AND THEN WE WERE THERE.

WEIRD, I THOUGHT.

THIS KID WAS MY AGE WHEN HE DIED.

IN MEMORY OF
JOHN
SON OF DANIEL AND SARAH KNAPP
WHO DIED
MARCH 25TH, 1766
AGE 12 YEARS

BUT I WAS *ALREADY* RUNNING.

JERRY! THEY'VE *GOT* ME!

IT WON'T LET GO!

WE WERE BOTH *TRAPPED.*

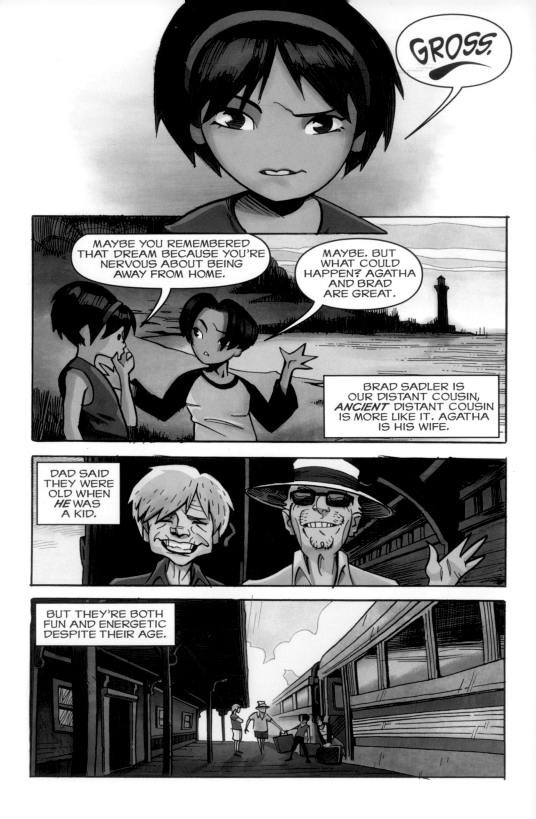

WHAT'D YOU DO *THAT* FOR? I WAS JUST WEASELING SOME *GOOD* STUFF OUT OF THEM.

SOCK

CAN'T YOU *SEE?* IT'S JUST ANOTHER DUMB JOKE.

THERE'S NO GHOST.

DESPITE THE HEAT, A CHILL RAN DOWN MY BACK.

WAS THERE A GHOST?

DID I REALLY WANT TO FIND OUT?

OVER DINNER, WE TOLD AGATHA AND BRAD ABOUT SAM, NAT, AND LOUISA.

THEY SAID THEY KNOW YOU.

YEP. *NEIGHBORS.*

WERE WE REALLY GOING TO TRAP A GHOST TONIGHT?

WHAT IF THE ROCKS WON'T *BUDGE?* WHAT IF WE SLIP AND *FALL?*

WHAT IF THE GHOST *DOES* FLOAT OUT?

WE'RE IN *DEEP* TROUBLE NOW. ALL *FIVE* OF US!

READY?

WE'LL WAIT DOWN *HERE.*

MY LEGS FELT RUBBERY AS WE CLIMBED THE DAMP ROCKS.

IF THE GHOST COMES OUT, WE'LL *DISTRACT* HIM.

ONE *SLIP* WOULD CAUSE A ROCK SLIDE... AND THE GHOST WOULD *KNOW* SOMETHING WAS UP.

WHAT'S *WRONG?* WHY ARE THEY WAVING?

111

113

115

118

WE PEERED UP AT THE CAVE AND WAITED.

NO ONE CAME OUT.

IT WAS *OVER.*

MYSTERY *SOLVED.*

WHERE *WERE* YOU?

BRAD AND I WERE WORRIED *SICK!*

IT'S KIND OF A LONG STORY ...

START AT THE *BEGINNING.* THAT'S USUALLY THE BEST PLACE.

TERRI AND I DID OUR BEST TO EXPLAIN THE WHOLE STORY.

122

AS WE TALKED, I COULD SEE THEIR EXPRESSIONS CHANGING.

WE'RE REALLY SORRY.

THE IMPORTANT THING IS THAT YOU'RE *SAFE*.

JERRY, *LOOK*. HARRISON SADLER'S *DOG*.

BARK!

BARK!

HE MUST HAVE ESCAPED AND *FOLLOWED* US–

BARK!

WHOA!

EASY, BOY. I'M YOUR *FRIEND*, REMEMBER?

BARK!

I'M NOT A...

...GHOST...

THE END

128

131

132

137

146

151

158